MIRRAN THOUGHT

MIRRAN THOUGHT
Spitzwiesenstr. 50
90765 Fürth
Germany

www.empty.de
empty@empty.de

READ THREE (MT-473)

Herstellung und Verlag:
Books on Demand GmbH, Norderstedt.
www.bod.de
info@bod.de

First printing 2006

ISBN 3-8334-4745-1

MIRRAN THOUGHT is the publishing arm of Mirran Threat, a company devoted to releasing the music and writings of the various members of Doc Wör Mirran. Mirran Thought and Mirran Threat are both divisions of MT Undertainment.

ALIEN PECKER

The complete
Doc Wör Mirran
series of writings,
Volume Two

Joseph B. Raimond

for Frank and Phil

Contents

All pieces written 2000 - 2005 by Joseph B. Raimond except "Ceddie Speeks" , "Habi Habi!", "Koofer Dyne", "Drowf Drooken" and "Twerp" which were written together with Cedric Joseph Raimond IV, without whom this book never would have been completed.

Special thanks to John Mervin and his friend Wylie for the title and inspiration for the piece "Wupr".

Front cover: "Alien Pecker"
Back cover: "Six Circles Help Define The Body"
Front and back cover art by Joseph B. Raimond, from the "Daily Plop" series, summer 2002

Meyow

Shitty kitty
Pisser n de flur

Wack, wack,
Splat gers de cat

Pur, pur
Buttol n de air
Air n me sup
Clods 'n berd

Wack, wack,
Splat gers de cat

Ern de tay
Bill, steel
Mi fud
Nerk dern
Mi cough
Fee

Wack, wack,
Splat gers de cat

Ruff, wuff,
Chas dug rend de
Hus, hiss, hisser

Wack, wack,
Splat gers de cat

Brest Burst

Brest burst
Kabloom, kabloom,
Bazoom

Spurtin' titty
Blud 'n gutz
Milk 'n spastik
Plastik
Fer booblin' googlin'
I'd
'Ol men wid
Litter ardunz
Ter slap up
Slag
Tungun' slurp
Erf de subway
Wallz

Biff Nekkid

Biff erz tuff!
Yell, yell
Kikker azz wid
Won erm
Ter
Twas blazin' er
Tuff twat
'N strut ern
By de schlongz
Seeg hylin
Er nekkidnes
Mess

Sownee

Ay, lerk ma!
Itser sownee!
Fuggin
Mulitnashunanalkerperayt
Wicksers
Vicky vermit 'n unzll
Wheez kin proove wheez
Write
Bert got mer buks
'N buks rul de werld
Still wheez getta mersidge
Fer yew:
Eet shat!

Bellamie Brazeers

Wheezm gool'ol
Cerntry fulk
Plunk, plunk, twang
Kermeer ma, eet yer
Vittles

Wheez singum serngs bert
Bigg boobs, er jugz
'N bier sluggin'
Fister wavin' merons
Piker-uper trucks
'N kow dung onums
Breth

Ferk de sitty sliker
Typums, de kern't no
Milk ner cerw
Ner wanna pop
Er own kin fulk

Jak Keroo Quak

Ers bein' boner rud agin
Munchin' meez tashun
'N swigin' sudz

Stumbl inter er
Legend
Widda pen ina
Mee hand
Ana stank boner
Breth

Test Eez

Swing, swing
Fromer Swinger
Sackze perlee
Lick
Wid
Gerna nok yew
Upper
'N lay
Yew dern

Gerna multy
Ply
Mee
Spee
Seez

Merreed

Meer izer
Merreed, 'n herpeed
Bert it

Red herd
Perty gurl 'n all
Shmoozin' ener bak seet
'N hickods ern me
Nek

Rome
Ants
Izer biggum
Pert me live

Ayez bein
Reedy
Fer luv

Wupr

Wershed up,
Punque rawker
Wheez being chekered inter
De 'ol folks humfer
Wuprz

Wheez tryin 'n dyin'
Ter pogo
'N slamb
Buttner wheelch
Hairz
Bein' tyin' us dern

Wheez bummin' change
Lik all good crusties do
Do
'N be stinkin' uper sterm
Shert fer owl graves

'N de yungunz
Dayz dinkin `wheez
Bin too ol' fer um 'core
Butt wheez bein' de
Hardest ov
De hard
Shert fer owl graves

Blessin'

Tis a tit
Blessin'
Demen boobs frum
Bess
'N
Her boosen
Buttie
Hammin' iter
Uppititty
Butt
Titty
Smellum
Titty
Sawcee
Bess
Isser
Lecker 'n
Licker
'N muncher
Er
Loos
Berncin'
Boobums
'N ways
Reedy
Fera
Goodum
Bums
Blesser

Sperashun

Blub, blub
Dripper drabble
Shmeer 'n pook
Scrapee all dem
Sperashun
Ert ter can
Vase

Show de werld
Yer nack fer
Licititty
Widder allyer
Ree
Vews 'n writerups

Butt
Her mee,
Eyez bein' herm 'n
Werkin
Fer
F art
Izzer mer
Als de
Sperashun

Bubbl

Blib blab, bubbl
Snip snap, snubbl
Gib gab, grubbl

Mrip mop, mumbl
Flip flop, fumbl
Plip plop, puddl

Snip snap, snubbl
It at, uttl
Crip crap, crabbl

Drip drab, dribbl
Zip zap, zappl
Frip fart, fumbl

Grit gross, grumbl
Hip hop, humbl
Yip yap, yumbl

Jet joe, jerkl
Whip wop, wobbl
Tit tat, turtl

Nip nap, nippl
Oop up, appl
Rip rig, rumbl

Carnap

Whorl carnap
Napped iniz car
Iz
Pirots karulized elatically

Ee sherd
Bee mer
Carfull
Nexterm

Pimmel Pummel

Swing swing
Thrak splat
Erch! Don
Beet upm pummel
Mer peter!
Ernly ich kern beet off'm
'N er licks me be'er den
U
Fer eez bein' smilin' fer mee!

Tella Stella

Stella book
O der
Onna shelf, 'n
Bee kwickie
Bert it
Fe de fires bea
Freezin', de woonds
Bein' deer
Sterms be fair, 'n
De deths bein'
Livin'

Mee rural
Vains
Bein' fulla royal
Oft blud
Mee teers perrin'
Outta ass ink

Fer persper
A
Shun
Fer mee book

Tella stella
Ter
Fuk off

Aus F Art

Brumm, brumm
Vroooom, spurt

Wheez muvin' ner
Fister dande
Bull it ferm a gun
Fister dan
Ever one

Wheez flyin' dernde
Erto bun

'N whence wheez
Rive
Mersn outta onna
Aus
F art
Wich wheez
Amis
Luv ser much

Eavy Ettal

Ard!
Arder!
Ead bangin'
Pimpl pusset nerd fagz
Vergins ter boot
Air gitarin more
Onz
Ich stomperin'
Ner yer collectiv
Samplung fakup blud
Depps
'N spit yer ut azer
Trutha wut yerz wirklich
Er,
Nix

Ox'n Ox

Slammer, bum
Wheerser 'ardcor nuw
F art erund fer uld ferts
Lick us
Imp Tea yer ernly
Ox'n idear
Eyzle win, er 'wayz do
Whirl yewz 'n
Blakoid kin ess
Eech uthers arses
In essen
Munch, chow
Slam

Pumbleshnook

Yerra shnook 'n 'oller
Urld fert fer 'n
Wank 'n wot not
Pipl' munch yer pumb
'N bee rite doin' so
Wheez allun Joes
Ernna de ladz
Seite

'N sters, shnooks, 'n
Woplz kin fukerf

Meez pectay
Shuns
Bein' grate

Fer Gott Ten

Aiz bee lerst
De luv uv heave
Ens er ne'er shern
Ern
Mai nerfs 'gin licks
Dey dert im sommer
Sev'ty nein
When de lite sherned
Ser brite 'n wheez
Wer ginter liv, luv
Fe'er
Bert ner wheez erl a
Nermal 'n such ass
Wheez gittin long im
Yeers
Meez lite done bein'
Blak fer times
Eyez reed er 'hartha
'N luved im
Bert stiny isser too
Strong
Ter wid 'n stand
Ser mi lite dern
Sting guished
'N ee bee
Fer gott ten

Hore

Slammer bumen de ayer
Newte, yer
Bimbern 'n slimmey
Up yer limey beder
Fulla jizm,
Hundert sorten
Yer nowen wert
Eech 'n ever
Tastee de testee
Ern dern fergit
Yersis also a
Moofie star!

Ugsum

Yerziz bein'
Mittee ugsum
Lertly ferin' meez
Ter bee
Holdin'

Loavesum
Berlooney loaf
Ferna fatso uglod
Buttergly toad bich
Widder perm-nent
Likee dykee
Wok
'Ner smell itter
Titter yer boobs
Deyzee bee 'angin'
'N anglinn ter pointin'
Süd

Profi Dunce

Werzitz destintittied
Ferde budder life ober in dem
Der
Hillsun yon
Ober der greet see
'N splash up yer quackers
'N puree
Tons
Fer de mangle de land 'n
Unger pins fer
Nuttin'

'N werl yer tatit
Killer fewum dem 'ol
Injuns fer me too
Dayziz nert much budder
Dan er dam vermint
Soweeso

Fubar

Bugger yer
Bumfodden
Smakem' inder sack
'N frigginert shite
Yer bumfugger mama
Yer sickle izer mite
Bit small 'n er boobs
Gergantchoowan

Meezle sword yerl
Stake, den fert it
Thru der pussy jok
'Ella, fubb wazit
Ter callit a
Queynte ert all yer
Dumshat

Wheez votin fer
De good 'ol
Dick
Aniyerall day

Fondl

Fondl mer nutz
'N wiffle mee sak
Lemme waf
Mer dik inner wind
Lemme pisser ernyer
Budz
'N stompl ernyer
All
Bine-o

Eyez
Kin maker
Cum lowdlee
Inn ner tim
Widda 'eavy
Pet
Inn 'n
Inn 'n ert
`N shakum
Lick a leef
Onya tree
Meez bein'
Ecks
Pert
Fondler

Zang, Dum Dum

Zang,
Dum dum
Wheez de few
Cher
'N wheez be cum

Zang,
Dum dum
Nerdsical dum
Shat
Killer man, bum
Feenda
Nazoid scum

Zang,
Dum dum
F art fer sum
De saika fun
Budder, kill inner hart
Mum

Exdro Fart

Wer, lukit mee, eey be
De bigges 'n
Bess

Bigges balls 'n prik
Prik me head
Slammin' all day
'N brag um butt fumbler
Sposic spass
Tik
Eetum up pussees
Teel de wurl
Wadder stud
Ee bin

Terk luts but in
See
Crit
Mee lonlee 'n mouth bigger
Dan me act
Shuns
Wishin'

Talkin' hid factoid
Meez fraid to show
Real
Titty

Introv Art

Aya frends 'n feends
Lemme intro
Truse
Mee sulf

Mee bein' lika
Turtl, wanna jess crall
Up 'n hid mee ead ina
Sand

Don lookit mee!

Mee feelin's bein' hurtin'
Fer de luv dat poors thru
Mee pores
Wishin' yew way inna river
Da neglect
Fer mee bin snot
Not cool nuff
Fer angin' ert at
De cerner joe cool lik

Don yakit mee!
Don think a mee!

Meez nert werth it
A lonlee ert fer all a tern
Titty
Ne'er kin stop starin'

Dee wonder de luv 'n
Boobs er perf
Ick
Shape

Wheez jes don get nuff
Slam 'n sweets
Jes don gots wat it takes
Layed 'n mornin', fuk
Fuker ne'er more
Budder ert dat
Bigger dan de wurl
Comp
Ass
Etern
Titty fer yew tee dwell pon
Lon fer mee
Ded

Die An

Yew
Callup me up
Atma mama
Dera jernee
Gans
Wuzza god lookin'
Twat 'n boss 'mam
Sheeya lookit mee
Ups 'n down lik
Widda goo goo
Eyez
Ballez
Sheeya watum mee!
Hello
Weenee
Magin
Airee slam, undressa
Mee widda goo goo eyez
Ballez
'N getter invit
Two er partee
Bert farce partee
No um chance
Ferda chance
Terra git inna
Die an

Ipso Fatso

Flumpa yer myle
Widda arse innya
Sow fa
Turdl roun
Fert 'n belcha
Lika swine in yer
Vains
Fukkin' uppa
Yer lif 'n da liffa
De kid
Fowl 'n layzee arse
Scusez
Wanna der werl butta
Don wanna werk
Yerra bring de artsa
Fett arse toowa
Perfect
Shun

Joice

Yo,
Jaimee
Wherum yew steel mee
Dea, yerra god
Dam
Theef
Yeder sagt, eyza too
Slim
Lar
Buttum eyez nebber
Laid mee eyez
Onya
'For

Yerza bilt
Um sowas liker
Time sheen

Real
Titty, yer
Notta even bern
Yit

Glub Dub Drib

Erna voy
Age nach lap
Uta wheez takin' time
Ter chekum up his
Story
En wa wheez fine?
Wert vree man reddy nows,
Bein' dat man
Kind iza heep a bull
Shat 'n wasta time,
Gerd fer nuttin' buncha
Loosers 'n f art bumz reedy
Ter steel yer dame 'n dope
Ter shoot yer inna back
Side wherl doin' deema
Faif
Or
Bastard wrech, wheez
Bilt ur wurl onna lies a
Crooks

Stirk

Stirk!
Stirk, stirk, stirk!
Mee bumsa bleedin'
Stirk!
Outta vrey ole iza
Black shit
Stirk, stirk, stirk!
Mee pee bee blud
Mee hirn bee mach
Stirk!
Mee don now
Wer ish bin
Stirk!
Mee bin fast
Tot
Stirk!
Stirk, stirk, stirk!
Lemme die
Stirk!

Der Tchimmee Page

Wang wang, soulee
Edd bangin' yer wanna
Beez
Gloree us, eego
Stuk up, hi nowz
Weez all waitin' fer der
Soulee

Meez hart ain't init
Waydin fer der 'perashun
Dattl nefer cum
Dull edd bangin' wanna
Shakum bunz bunneez
Blow yeez bak staige
Perm nokkers
Ain't no 'perashun wurth

Schmuk

Schmuker fuk, eet mee dump
Dump truk schmuker fuk suk
Eeler mist yer dash widda
Riprok hum bugger
Bum sukker

Wowee joesm, yer spired
Day fer sucha schmuk
Whir dir fallout leef ee
Smurter er wot?

Butt erl still no chans
Fer a lick a
Shun, bub
Yer jest ain't gots it

Sowee ill sow mer
Tadurs shoffelin'in
Brin fud,
Ser ter speek
In nert auf gebben
Bism ee mee lish,

Schmuk

Fett Sack

Fett rowls
Blubber bum swetin'
Drip drip stink
Flab rowls 'lectin'
Sludgee

Jumbin' jerks
Nockers nockem
Hous dern
Flab slappin'
Rumbl fuk

'Gustin'
Idjit
Fett sack

Tung Thrust

Red blister son
Shine, pukker
Puss lemmee
Lickem sex
Luv

Ayee, nert awl bad,
Mee
Kin rafe 'n see
Lik rom antz
Fuzee feelin'
Staree aiz, ead
Inna cluds 'n
Riddin' hi

Fera fect
Shapped red un
Lips finner den
Win, mee kin
Die fer, sucha

Yera Spaz

Spitter, spat
Blat
Shakup 'n quak
Kwake 'n shake
Piss yer pants
'N fert un cum
Trolled
Rumbloid widda ai
Ballz de buldj, nert
Member a ding
Buttz lookit funny
Aye

Twit Twat

Shak emup boobs
Yeah!
Waddel wuss, flippemup
Buns 'n jugz er
Oppin' 'n grindin'
Wallop upsidz de
Ead, stars 'n bulge
Wheez guyz all be
Slobbrin' 'n
Droollin' fer yer
Twat 'n ole
Ter stuffem up
Swett
Slime
Joos
Cum

Bert
Gray madder
Nert felt ner
Seem

Hundy Bundy

Vow vow, schnapp
Wagger wagger
Grintz
Certie pie, schnuggl
Maydee

Yerza burk, burk
Vow, 'n wagger
Rund de wurl
Droppen airs, turds
Wisser fronta de
Omaz

Chassem kitty
Upper baum
Vow,
Schnapper, wagger

Bee mee li'ul
Trulee,
Layloid

Rooch Roober

Scuse mee
Erm
Kinner yewz,
Rooch amol
Roober goober
Make way fer
Da big cheezum
Ead oncho
Boss man

Ner?
Wella er bout
Roochen roober
Ann how?

Meezum lik
Terd a standin'
Stand? Liker
Meez bones be
Akin
Sera bee apal
'N
Rooch

Yera Peon

Erl werld, con
Kerer ov
De peon redz
Lika spikey thru
De groinoids
Dess a
Mate um widda
Veerus, 'n sick
Ness un such
Steel der rich
Esses den be
Heddem widda grin
Licka backs tabbin'
Un gehoyer
Meez not prud
A mee her
Tadge

Rukkee Tsuckee

Ayy!
Urry up yer wanker
Wadds takin' ser lung
Widda werk yer lassee
Ass fuker muck
Wheez gonna shitter
Ya new 'ol
Waddsa dat!, wheez
Bein' urfull snotty
An wot
Meez prudda me
Stink tank, licka
Pro fester, lick
Widda buffoon paper
Ter 'ang anna wall
Lick ter da pussees
Dey bein' cummin'
In me fiss, 'n cummin'
When yer now wot ee
Meen!!
Ar ar!
Widda kwickeez
Rukkee tsuckee, lick
Now wastin' timber
Gonna nockem up
Kwik lick!

Wiz

Maka wiz
Taka dump,
Flerp up yer 'nsids, growler
Likka unger bum
Wizza a ver de seet
Yer swine!
Likka bus stashun
West woom
Wher yer
Lern yer manners,
Ya pig

Der stinka leeva
Cold, 'n rechin
Whatsa dee
Sees yer got
An' how?
Wher yer maka wiz
Meez void
Likka plaig

Leks Iss

Jammin' man!
Wheez bee rokin'
Ert de damp erl
Room fer
Sernds dey be er
Hart
Risin' fer er ops
'N dreems a cupla
Star ee aug
Yung unz widda weerd
'Tars
Anna wonder wanda
Fera fuk anna drum
Solo
De booz bein' flow
In 'n out, wheez ridin'
Hi
Skitzo 'n reedy ter
Plummet
Ter man, 'n
Kids 'ner day
Tim jerb

Elloid Ooglee

Grate
Googlee mooglee!
Its de elloid ooglee!
Cumin' ter shat ern
Yer day
Cumin' ter spoil
Yer brew
Ern eet yer pin
Yons too!

Widda sen
Dalo depp in tow
Eeza slippin'
Ona fett smudgees
Anna rolling de
Blubber hinter
Her, alde while
Ee steels yer
Blind

De elloid ooglee
A monster cunta
Slapper stink
Yer inna ground widda
Oogliest farce inna
Werl

Jazz My Azz

Spiegel spiegel,
On de wand
Whoo's de dumest
In de land?

Wy, youz bein' de
Dumest, fer me is shur
Eeza ripped ye off
Lemee tell yer, sur

Eeza youzed fer iz gain
Anna letyer paid de bucks
Anna ween yew neeted eem
Denz yew were fuked

Eeza let yer standin'
Enna blink de aye
Wid not a touht
De freend ship die

Ee kin mongo, shake
'N cat 'n throb
Ee will youz yew 'gin
Kaus dat eez job

Eeza ass hole, now it
As gold iz pur
End it ner
Nur dan is sure

Likity Split

Faster denna
Bullet fruma gum
Ich bin faster
Den anyone

Kwik her denna
Blinkin a de aye
Likka flash yer
Kin mizmee
Goin' bye

Aima butt fumbler
Riskin' me jaw ferra
Feel, aima nerf herder
Seeda patcha yunguns
Widda skweel

Erm goona poot
A flam 'n riss de roost
Erm goona flatch a
Pile a kwikee jooce

Imma hi on de hog
'N will life ferever
Likity split, imma man
Dat neber say neber

Wom

Womblz jam out, man!
Shure
Wheez be rockin' now ter de heep
Anna naz reth be gettin' dern
De rok keller on de prowl
Fer pussee 'n bier, pantin
Gray aired 'n doppey
Chekin' ert de new
Heiten
'N fillin' de raks
Widda sheenen temmas

Butt whee don got ridda
De tyrant, en good!
Ee be rottin' in somma sell
Burned by iz own greed
Ee be 'urtin'
Widda butt likin' baldee fert
Addiz side, lappin' de shat
Um iz ass

Butta times war not all bad
De promo tish fer sample
Got ussa droolin' fer free
Bees, widda cashunal find
Butter still glats over
Butter wombl tilla die

Injun

Bo wo wo wo
Tomma hawk up yer bum ferra
Tru scalper
Widda wigwam ferra wonung
Wheez respectya, yanow!

Retreet terra mud
Hutt
Butt,
Wheenya gotta wee
Dont yer dare pee
In de tee
Pee

De brafe ist brafe enuff
Ter tect iz
Skwa
Butt eel trade er ferra
Puffa da pees pipe
Anna chompa de magick
Shrooms

Hanf Manf

Eetemup schmoe
Weeee!
Gonna ride em up hi
Floot uber der wolkens
Red ai wida
Munchees,
Gotta gobbl up all de grub
Den burf it all raus in techno
Color, message ter god onna
Big white tel
Phoney
De roach be grawlin'
Way, widda my fer
Stand

Pee Nuß

Emma gittin' up in der worl
Er hard loolit round
Knobin' widda chiks
Meßin' rund widda hole
Crowd
Eetem up peter, cumin'
Rund widda lookin er
Eyez ter da sowl
Wheeza sowl 'lated
Widda perfect fit
'N whenna dickz gon
Shee bee
Lookin' sad lik
Widda no full
Fille ment
Shee bee smart too boot
Widda red lit 'n
Bigga boosen, snap 'er man!
Bakina bush, erm fer good!
Swingers,
De nutz be swingin' in de
Breez

Tug

Dern tug me up at nine
Pee em
Radder, tug me down 'n ert
De ganse nite lung
Widda ruckin' toons
Man

Wheeza be buddees 'n
Booz guzzle brows
Wheeza elp eech udder
Ut

Wee Willie Winkie

Erts singin' de dum jokes
Wheez bein' dum funded
Wasted widda whif a
Babee doo
Meth wold ifee could
Butt ee kernt, so ee
Left to pun a jab
Back ter de brits
Saleem said sai yon
Ara, dood
En let iz nose no where it
Goos
Slimee drops ter drip yer
No funktional pensil
Utensil
De brits shooda left long
Bee fer dey did
De mid nite
Chil cum frema
Day brake, kama
Sutra boner

Artimus

Yo, art
I mus pile yer
Poop over ter
Lennards skin
Yard, wheez gerna
Rock 'n roll over ter
Bammi, sweet ome
Bart aizl tellya, yer
Not no free
Boid, yersa suddern
Redneck hik bummfuk
Yokl dattl squeel widda
Publicans 'n jerk
Offa sudden bap
Tits wanker weenie
All de whil he prays
Ter iz lord jeezus
Caddy lack
Balls 'n bummer
Wanna onlee tak
Yee fer a ride
No whatcha
Meen?

Rex Dildo

Ker splat
Gers der cat
Widda smile all de way down
Ena swoon fer de ladeez
Eeza croonin' ena folks
Muzak ell

Wheeda all butt iz
Al
Bums,
Ner iza tsait
Ter pay home
Age ter de grate
Sex toi

Sherve it!
Woo
Man!
De rex bein' slim
Ee, stiff aza
Bord deez daze

Rex dildo
Iza stiff
Fer ever

Kween

Gerd safe der
Kween
Der lord all
Limee, has dern cum

Wher all ben safed
Ter hale der kween

Wee Nee

Lemmee bite unto thou art
Wee Ner
Uskar,
Yerz bein' dribblin chup
En turd
Ferra swine paked unto
Iz own poop shoot
An wherz the chili?
Dern fergit de warm
Buns, nuthin' bedder
Cuss id still luv ter be
Ern usker meyer wee ner

Hoodlumz Baddl

Werda crips ern werda shits
Wheez bein' riddy ter
Kik yer arse

Erna baddl de bluds
Dey no bros ter uz,
Cuz
Werda crips ern werda shits

Wheebee pushin' drugz
En thugz, yewbee payin'
Per tection
Cuz,
Werda crips ern werda shits

Werda stoppers ferda
Coppers, dey be givin' us time
Wheez be layen em cold
Cuz,
Werda crips ern werda shits

Bill Ee Odol

Ee git
Yer stunkin' up de
Skunk
Wherz ya odol, idol?

Wee bee
Jammin' ter yer X
Wheerza yew be smellen
Up de wy
How cumz
Yer a rich punque
Widda dow, butt yer
Kint spara buk fera
Rowl on

Wadda Hadda Do De Da

Wadda hadda do de da, daddi?
Hadda daddi ana doo doo da?
Daddi hadda doo doo da drooben,
Da

Doh!

Slurm

Slurp dem slurm sudz
Belchem up slurm slime
Dribbl de goo slurm slime rite
Stumbl en berf, up de chuk
Slurm inna fyewtch er
Ramma lamma
Ding dong

Munni Punni

Yers en yers go, luv
Inner ayes ena dee zeez
Inner self, shee wuz mee
Luved munni

Erwayz cooked de munni
Punni fer er liddl won
En gived mee de munni
Wader swell, widda
Bubbels

Er now seez gone
Ser munni yers
Bert wayz imma
Hert

Enna dreem aher
Enna feel er waitin'
Fer me

Dood

Dud
Watzup, dood!
Watz happn, man!
Erl jez eet yer liv
Er, widout yer cryin!
Lik, dood

Er, ger fuk uff
Yer kweer faggut dud
Dood, yers a beein
Feelin me up fere an
Asswhip, wipe

Dud, whatcha up wer
Wat say

Fuckelberri

Fin, azz in

Em aye es es
Aye es es
I pee pee
Eye

Git ern dern de
Ribber bote red nek shite
Eed, glubber long dem
Slud banks widda
Grass inna tuth, en lookin
Kool, dood

Stra at erna jugga
'Shine fer wenna niters
Git only enna hot
Mantic lik, der mond
Gernin dern de ribber

En wheez dinkin
Bert de gert
Anna goona
Di

Bee Pee

Kwuit derding up me
Err, yer terds,
Fulla gas en furts
Wheez gonna chev er fists
Up yer ron wenna yer dernt
Stop widda, yer ess o
Gonna nock yer blok uff,
Aldi way ter shell

Bullerjan

Werm my up, yer
Bull, brenn stuff ferra
Lite, kep dis haus
Hot, lick her up
Snuggl werm, eetem up
Holz ern wud, ferra tom
Kreeg wheez ill leb oober
En ert last de next eis
Aig, wicher cum zoom nuff
Wen all de anders wil freez
Unzer jan willern werm up
Uz fer de spell, kold
Wheezl uddle en lersten
Ter de crap an popple
Der rauch ern smuk
Will stin uns eyez, bert
Wernt cure, cuz itz all be
Caidded up, ern wheezl
Leb oober

Ay Titti

Ay, titti
I, titti
O, wat u do to me

Wera goen down sud
Ter de titti see
Wera gonna wach dem
All little wunders goen
Bouns de buns

Lotza skin, un
No iddy biddy, teenee weenee
Polka dot bikinees
Ter dy loot
De loot

An de pommes
Er all cumin' frum de
Pommersfeld

Banana Boobed

Pernty yet ferm,
Widda under full fase ter match
Dey all maid funna her
An onli eye newed how
Bute ee full she reely wuz

An she wanted de dork
Fer godz saik!

Fukindumshatrednekarshole Pert Too

Hay yuewwz!
Wert! Yer still 'angin' rund ere?
I sherda pownded yer skull inder
First time, yer lung aired ippy
Cummie
Pinko fag

Will nowz ya gots it cummin,
Ern a mess itel bee ver yer
Momma ter cleen up
Fter yer go runnin' 'ome

Cuz yer no, weez dernt tol
Rate yer kind in deez ere
Perts

Weezer gawd feerin' volk
Up ere in deez ere
Perts

Ern wera gonna kik de
'Ell owda yew!

Terd Citee

Wheezer goin' ter
Terd citee

Yep, wer livin' in
Terd citee

Er ganse werl is 'trolled
In terd citee

Der doggee terds, kleb on
Mer feet
Der kittee terds, eyez gots
Ter scrape of der pan
Der babee terds, mes gots
To change twice a day

Terds be runnin' me live
Day in en day ert
Ern me nows wanna move
Kwik, lik
Butt, tis de way ov live
'Ere in turd citee

Booky Boo

Ay, booky boo
U kyooty u
Whatcha sayin' ter me
Yer ol' daddy ow

De bumsty backen
Er glowin' widda glee
Ay 'appy blowney lofe
Ern yer bringin'
A lite aner teer
Termee ayez

Ern endloss freulich
Keit, anna babbl widda
Pure hart, pure butee

Sayin' mor dan most
Uvus kin say inna
Lif tim

Yers got me gotten cot
Rapped roun yer lil finner
In I won let yer down

Yama Ha Ha

Twing, twung, twang, twong
Plink, plank, plong
Vroom, vroom
Thrak

Wheez gonna git yer back

Jam, man,
Jam 'er up
Wherza band, wher
Gonna rok!

Wheez gotter zeug
Pro fee too!
Wheeza jammin'
Anna rokin' u!

Alien Pecker

Dey met inder
Bar, alien en all
Iz gleeming three eyz
Bulgin' wid lust
Undressin' er slowlee

She led him feel er up
Wid iz all for arms,

De first arm strokin' a tit
De secund grabbin' de udder
De turd arm fumlin' er butt
De forth arm pokin' erna pokin'

All tryin' er oles
One adder time

Sher jus sayed,
Beem me down
Ern fuk me 'ard
Gimme yer lowd
Frum de
Alien pecker

Dey roked en dey rolled
En she screemed wid de'
Lite, eech time ee cum
Skweertin' de lowd
From de
Alien pecker

Mey Ghun

Uhn uhn,
De mey ghun
Blows de see uttle
Grunge fuk
Soodow punk
Cuz ee put out a
Sub poop rekid
Udda munth

Ay, mey ghun
Yer stoopid cow
Izza blobbin' up de seet
Turning de eMpTy inter
A joke

Fuk uff en dye!

Kaak!

Wherza gonna rok de haus dern
Sadda
De pointed won widda
Gittar

Az gitter god
Eezun der best
Gawd dern inde stat
Eeza ertist
Fer kris sake
Ern ee serves sum
Spect!

Enna band izza
Jammin'
Er horn widda
Sow lows
De drums enna base
Widda back beet,
Alla gerna
Rock er sox off
Ter nite!

Moo Kow

Der fermer
Creeped roun' de creep kows
Ern tested de tits widda
Twong

Ee cummed up ter
Hell ga
De talkin' kow
Unda traid ter milk de
Udder

De kow was lick
Impashent
Ern scolded boi fermer
"Not dis udder yer dummer
Tis de udder udder"

Hello, Weenie

Hello der,
Whatz dat yer tryin' ter
Scared me wid?

Wha? Da little weener
Stink
Sposd der make me shitter 'n
Shake?
Dat little stiffie
Ez not werth de
Budder

Kern't scare er brownie
Widda dat
Kern't scare yer momma
Widda dat
Kern't eben scare yer
Trickser treeters
Widda dat

Sey be ringin' der door
Bell, ern yer anser widda lidder
Weenie stink 'angin'
Ert

Ern wheezl all come yellin'
Hello, weenie!

Shitler

Ferk uff,
Yer baldee hedded,
No braned broots
Wheez dern need yer kind
In deez 'ere perts

Ger back ter yer beer
Belching, dumshat
Hoolgans
Ern pund eech udder

Eyez taka stance, man
Ern shout natzees raus,
Uni feel it frum me soll

Ders a reeson
Wa rum yer sherts er brown
An' it cum from yer leeder
De biggest turd ever to be shat
Shitler 'imself

Geschwabbl

Blubber butt, yer
Ooglie fat towd
Airry dum shat
Widda hauffn chins

Yer waddle twaddle rund
De layers de fat
Schwabblin' rund
Stinkin' n droopsee boobs

Yer kin only rowl
Ter de next fast food
Joynt
Stuff it all in, pig!
Belch en furt
Musick ter yer fat eers

Disnee land waiber

Frankenboobies

Lertsa flesh,
Slumpin' sholders, backsa
Akin'
Wat kinna doo
Ter stand stait

Lettem at me
Widda nife
Lettem at me
De boobs be ripe

Cuttem up
Pullit ut
Stitch em up

Lookit in de speegel
Ima patchwork puzle
Eers its 'angin'
Der its urts
Eysa lookin like
En frankenboobs

Ceddie Speeks

Da!
Da!

Grap grap
Mamamamam
Mama
Mama
Da!

Giga
Giga
Giga!

Da!

Dakadakadaka
Grap grap
Nemma
A?
A?

Habi Habi!

Giga wawr wawr
Giga!
Owa giga
Uberall giga

Efanenene
Affe, o o o o
Kaze, meow
Auto, brm brm
Booch
Andre booch

Shokade
Habi habi
Haben
Kookee
Habi habi
Haben!

A kornee
Pi conee
Aa ai
Habi

Payn
Eisenban
Shu shu
Habi
Eisenban
Haben!

Koofer Dyne

Bonk, ouwwaa!
Kekik koofer dyne
Ouwwaa makt

Splash, krash
Sowerii makt
De wadder
Ist ge koofer dyned

Shuv, krash
Giga!
Audo, bus
Ist ge koofer dyned

Didg Eree Doo Doo

Hrooooommmmmm
Hroooooooommmmmmmm
Hroooooooooooommmmmmmmm

Flatch, stinker
Ugghhh!
Grows

Hrooooommmmmm
Hrooooooooommmmmmmmm
Hroooooooooooommmmmmmmm

'Roo turds
Flerchem enna yoober all
Ferts enna stink
Butta wheeza kin immer bee jammin'
Una didg eree doo doo!

Hrooooommmmmm
Hroooooooommmmmmmmm
Hroooooooooooommmmmmmmm
Wheeza jammin'!

Drowf Drooken

Ish will drowf drooken
Gegic will drowf drooken
Bing! Bing!

Dadee,
Nain! Hoch hayben
Bing machen
Gegic will drowf drooken

Etz daa!
Gegic hat owaa gemacht
Gegic had gewaiynt
Gegic will drowf drooken

Twerp

Aya liddl man
Wassa mache da du da?

Rum rennen
Koofer dyne
Hai ya machen
Bussi geben
Owwa machen
Danzen urren
Lowfen!

Yer lidle blowney lowf
Kermeer

Lidl

Oops, brewskis aggi
Mussa roober rennen
Teda lidl en koofen mir
Ne paar sydla

Oder soll ish
Te de aldi gehn
Essa bilger alsa comet
Butta de abshaum dee
Da rum rennt

Oder gehma teda edeka
Deez habns aber alle zug macht
Soo teuer warz soweeso

Oder farma nach ploos
Enna shnappen unza paar
Kleinna prysa

Na!
De hund muss rows
Alzo lowfa weer te da lidl
Enna kowfen unza paar
Sydla dow!

Eynz, zwo, dry, foonf
Enna lidl bitta mee
Enna lidl bitta yoo

Gegik

Kerm 'ere yer liddl twerpoid
Un wersh yer yow gert uffa yer mund, boi!
Yer be stinkin' wie er sow!
Gunna weksel dem ol' nappees fer shur, boi!

Dern be wackin' in der waddur,
Yerll catch kold un hafte vizit doc deets

Un stop hollerin' ata toppa yer lungs, boi
Er yers ti gow ter yer room

En kleen up yer leggos dammit!

En eet yer dinner boi!
No, yer cant hafta shokaade

Kerm eer sun,
Yer daddy doz luv u mer
Dan an ding on dis eer erth, boi!

Nomo

Mi grumpl
Brumbeloid tede max
Jers wanna how 'n mame
Puncher lites ert

Crawl weg 'n sub
Eer
Ert a town, statt
Viven lick er 'thal
Eezy lifer, jes
Getter fuk ert!

Nomo werk
Nomo luv
Nomo CRuD
Nome reebilly
Teez

Nomo

Burd

Ba ba ba
Burd, burd, burd,
De burd iza wurd

Ba ba ba
Burd, burd, burd,
De burd iza wurd?

Ooohuhhhhh, yeah!

Ba ba ba
Burd, burd, burd,
Dis burd iza nerd

Ba ba ba
Burd, burd, burd,
Dis burd iza nerd?

Ooooohuuuuuuuhhhhh, si!

Ma ma ma
Meow meow
Mama, mama,
Meow, meow, meow
Meow, meow
Didz cat eet de burd?

Ooohuuuuuhhhhhhhh, no!

Ba ba ba
Burd, burd, burd
De burd layda turd

Ba ba ba
Burd, burd, burd
De burd layda turd?

Ughhhh, ya!

Haber

Ha ha haber
Perfekt fera
Dumshat
Lick me

Meezle bum
Lernin'
Uber 'n uber agin
Butt
Ner lukyfuky

Depper dan a
Dernob

Bart bed
De
Lukin'

Dursh Fall

Ee git ee git
Erml wurz de kingoid
Er de chunks 'n
Bad smerls
Wheez nowzes
Bee hurtin'
Nickzonz eben frum
De sex feet
Ernder iz dribblin'
Ransid snot
Fer yer ooz
Kleen-em up joe
Izr wut yer alwiz
Dice
'N so fern
Azzer wuz yer inten
Shunz

Lerd Merth

Aye ersewip
Wachum were yer 'ing
Er'll pound yer dumbshat
Skull
Inter de pay
Ment, 'n make eet dert
Yer dreck
Sow
Bastardo
Werp
'N bum
Mofo

Jes yew
Wat'll aye
Kik yer ballzum
Ter der moon
Fetch um up yew
Erna dark street cerner
Mittle de nite
'N see yew
Swine

Swum

Wheez wernt'd te swum erund
Butt her wersn't ficked up ernuff
Shee letim dern, 'n ee
Wernted ter wein
'N cry iniz beer
De therts, man dey
Bean swummin' rend iz
Heed
What sherder der und so
De mangle una feeluns
Terd iz hart te kwit messin'
Widiz grau cellen
'N ser ee dun done sterted
Feelin' butt
Her

Cummie

Keeler
Cummie fur
Mummie

Redziz takin'
Old
Er de spirit
De nay
Shun
'N turnin' iter
Plum pud
Thing

Leeve um mee
Ter mi bucks
'N cash
Lemee bein' 'n stay
Er derler
I'd
Swine

Frijid

Eyez buggin' yer ter
No end, me no
Butter butts
Ger fleegen durch
Mi mind
'N bubblin' boobs
Er cheep feel izm
Bedder dan
Nuttin'

Butt shee
Bee slappin' me
Hand, wile
Eyes bee droolin'
'N gogo eyed

Butter
Shees bee
Sayin' nur no
Day inner ut
Day fter day
Ter nada fin
Immer 'n immer
Wide
Her

Depp Burple

Ow
Yew red
Die
Ter rok?!?!

Eyez sayed,

Ow
Yew red
Die
Ter rok ?!?!

Blaideez 'n wurms
Der fill
Mor werst iz prud
Der prevent
Life ern stayed,
Depp burple!

Twang, twang
Strut, strut
Fert, fert
Dum solo

"Smert, under
Wudder
Fer ina sky"